Once upon a time, in a faraway kingdom, a beautiful Princess was born.

The King and Queen were very happy.

They asked six fairies to be godmothers to the Princess.

3

The six fairies soon came to the castle. But there was also a seventh fairy.

She was very angry that she had not been invited to the party.

The King and Queen had forgotten her!

They asked her to join the party for the Princess.

SHORT TALES
Fairy Tales

Sleeping Beauty

Adapted by Shannon Eric Denton
Illustrated by Mike Dubisch

WAYLAND

First published in 2014 by Wayland

Copyright © 2014 Wayland

Wayland
338 Euston Road
London NW1 3BH

Wayland Australia
Level 17/207 Kent Street
Sydney, NSW 2000

Adapted Text by Shannon Eric Denton
Illustrations by Mike Dubisch
Colours by Wes Hartman
Edited by Stephanie Hedlund
Interior Layout by Kristen Fitzner Denton
Book Design and Packaging by Shannon Eric Denton

Copyright © 2008 by Abdo Consulting Group

A cataloguing record for this title is available at the British Library.
Dewey number: 823.9'2

Printed in China

ISBN: 978 0 7502 7829 4

Wayland is a division of Hachette Children's Books, an Hachette UK company.
www.hachette.co.uk

The first five fairies gave wonderful gifts to the Princess.

The first fairy gave her beauty.

The second fairy gave her great wisdom.

The third fairy gave her grace.

The fourth fairy made her a perfect dancer.

The fifth fairy gave her a beautiful voice.

Then the seventh fairy gave the Princess her gift.

She said a spindle would prick the Princess's hand and the Princess would die.

Then the mean fairy disappeared.

The sixth fairy still had her gift to give.

She could not undo the mean fairy's gift.

But she could change it so the Princess would not die.

Instead, the Princess would sleep for 100 years.

The King and Queen thanked the good fairies.

But they were still worried for their beautiful daughter.

The King commanded all spindles be forever removed from his kingdom.

The people thought this was a wonderful idea. Everyone was glad again.

The Princess grew into a beautiful young woman.

For almost 15 years the kingdom was happy.

Then one day, the Princess came upon an old tower.

She saw an old woman inside hard at work.

The Princess asked the woman what she was doing.

'I am spinning, my pretty child' said the old woman.

The Princess asked if she could try.

The kind old woman was happy to show her.

As the Princess took the spindle, the sharp needle pricked her finger.

The curse had come true!

The beautiful Princess was struck down.

The old woman cried out and people came from all around to help.

Everyone tried to wake the Princess.

But loud noises could not break the spell.

Water could not break the spell.

The King and Queen were very upset.

They knew their daughter must now sleep for 100 years.

The Princess was carried into the palace.

She was laid upon a bed.

She was beautiful even in her sleep.

No kingdom was ever so filled with sadness.

News of what had happened spread throughout the land.

It soon reached a dwarf in the kingdom.

The dwarf knew he must tell the sixth fairy.

But she was very far away.

The dwarf had a pair of magic boots.

In his magic boots he could cover many miles in one step.

He would get to the fairy in no time.

The dwarf told the fairy what had happened.

She thanked the dwarf and prepared to leave.

The dwarf ran home in his magic boots.

The fairy had her own magic.

She rode in a blazing coach pulled by dragons.

The fairy soon reached the castle.

The King and Queen took her to see their sleeping daughter.

She approved of everything the King and Queen had done.

The Queen asked what they should do next.

The fairy had an idea. She said the Princess would not be alone when she awoke.

The young fairy took out her magic wand.

She began to touch everyone in the palace!

She even touched all of the animals.

Everyone the fairy touched fell into a deep sleep.

All this was done in a moment.

But the young fairy still had more work to do.

The kingdom would need to be protected.

The fairy waved her wand once more.

Trees, bushes and brambles grew up all around the kingdom.

The Princess and her people would sleep safely for 100 years.

Outside the kingdom time passed.

New kingdoms arose.

For almost 100 years, all in the land was happy.

There was now a kind Prince who loved to explore.

He rode his horse all over his grand kingdom.

One cold spring day, he rode far beyond his father's lands.

The Prince was sure no one had ever come this far before.

He was alone in the darkest forest.

Then he spied five great towers through the thick wood.

The Prince had once heard a story of a lost castle.

There was a Princess who lay inside it.

He had never believed the story before.

The story said that only a Prince could wake the Princess.

He decided to see if it was true.

But he had no idea how to get through the thick forest.

Then the trees and bushes spread apart as if by magic.

The Prince saw an amazing sight.

All around him people and animals were stretched out sleeping.

The Prince entered a room at the top of the palace that was covered with gold.

On a bed rested the beautiful Princess.

The Prince touched her hand gently.

At that touch, the magic spell was broken. All the people and animals awoke.

The 100-year sleep was over.

The people began to celebrate.

Everyone danced, feasted and sang all night long.

The Prince and the Princess were married during the celebration.

They lived happily ever after.